W9-AVL-713

NICE TO MEET YOU...
AGAIN

Empowering children to find joy and understanding in loved ones with dementia

Written by Suzanne Bottum-Jones, RN

Illustrated by Aaron Boyd

LITTLE CREEK PRESS®
AND BOOK DESIGN

Mineral Point, Wisconsin USA

Little Creek Press®
A Division of Kristin Mitchell Design, Inc.
5341 Sunny Ridge Road
Mineral Point, Wisconsin 53565

Illustrator: Aaron Boyd
Book Design and Project Coordination: Little Creek Press

First Edition
March 2018

Printed in Wisconsin, United States of America.

For more information or to order books:
www.littlecreekpress.com

Library of Congress Control Number: 2018934538

ISBN-10: 1-942586-34-5
ISBN-13: 978-1-942586-34-0

National Center for
Dementia Behaviors Management

www.centerfordementiabehaviors.com

First and foremost, I would like to thank the wonderful people who have honored me by allowing me to provide them care in their journey of life. It is these brave friends, clients, and patients, who have taught me to "see" their needs and cherish their spirits regardless of their current circumstances.

Thank you to my family for their constant love, support, and encouragement; you are my daily inspiration.

Finally, thank you to my husband for loving me so completely for 28 years that I have thrived and flourished in a way otherwise not possible. It has been your love and sacrifice that has allowed me to spend my life loving and caring for others.

This book is dedicated to my dad with love.

DEAR READER,

As a nurse, I realize how challenging it can be to connect with those who are experiencing cognitive and behavioral changes associated with various types and stages of dementia.

My goal in writing this book is to help readers understand what might be going on with your loved ones' cognition and provide guidance and tools to set families up for successful interactions. Ultimately, I hope that families rediscover the joy in connecting with their loved ones despite the difficulties they may face daily, thereby preserving relationships.

With this book, I would also like to give a voice to those who are experiencing cognitive changes and who may no longer be able to express their needs. In doing so, I hope to help improve their quality of life, protect their dignity, and unmask the gifts they still have to offer.

I wish you peace, hope, and understanding as you travel this journey together.

—Suzanne Bottum-Jones, RN, BSN, MA
  (Director—National Center for Dementia Behaviors)

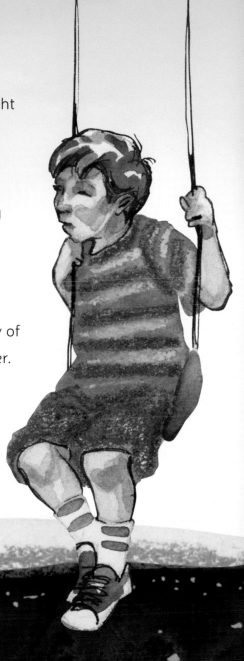

"No! No!" shouted Ollie as he ran into the park
next to the Memory Care Center.

"I don't want to go in there! That's not my grandpa;
he doesn't even know who I am anymore."

"Hi, Sofia," Ollie's mom said to the nurse walking toward her. "Well, here we go again."

"Oh dear," said Sofia. "Ollie still doesn't want to go in?"

"No. I wish I knew what to do," said his mom, Mary, as she returned Sofia's hug.

"I know it's hard on all of you, but it's very common to be frightened or upset when you see someone you love behaving so differently — even for grown-ups," Sofia explained. "Mary, would you mind if I talked with Ollie?"

"Please do," sighed his mom.

Sofia sat on the swing next to Ollie. "Hey, Ollie. I'm Sofia.
I work at this memory care center, and I'm a friend of
your Grandpa Walt."

"Really? Does he know who you are?" blurted Ollie.

"He doesn't always remember my name or face, but he knows
I'm a friend and someone who takes care of him," Sofia said gently.

"I don't know WHY he can't remember me. I'm his only grandson!"
Ollie looked down with tears in his eyes.

"Ollie, it can be very scary to see someone you love act this way.
But I also think it might help to understand what is happening
with your grandpa . . . and why."

"As we age, physical changes happen differently for each of us. Some of these changes we can see, like gray hair. Some of these changes we CAN'T see, like changes in the brain," said Sofia.

"If we can't see them, how do we know they happen?" asked Ollie.

"Well, there are people who study brains and these types of changes. Let me explain what they've found," Sofia said as she pulled out her cell phone. "Have you ever tried to call someone and you have no cell service, so your call won't go through, or your call drops?" asked Sofia.

"Our brains are made up of billions of little cells called neurons that all talk to each other, just like when our phone makes a connection. When our brain cells are all communicating, our brains work just like we want them to, and the conversation is crystal clear.

"But sometimes, when we get older, our brain cells can't talk to each other like they used to. This causes problems with someone's memory, thinking, or behavior called 'dementia,'" explained Sofia. "There are many forms of dementia, Ollie. Your grandpa has a memory-type of dementia, which is why he can't remember you."

"Can I catch dementia?" asked Ollie.

"No, it isn't a disease you can catch, like a cold," Sofia explained. "Also, keep in mind, dementia doesn't happen to everyone as we get older."

"Ollie, can I show you some of my friends who had the same kinds of questions and worries that you have about your own grandpa — and what they are doing to help?" asked Sofia.

"You mean I can help? I'm just a kid."

"Sure!" Sofia said assuredly. "You can be a great help to your Grandpa Walt."

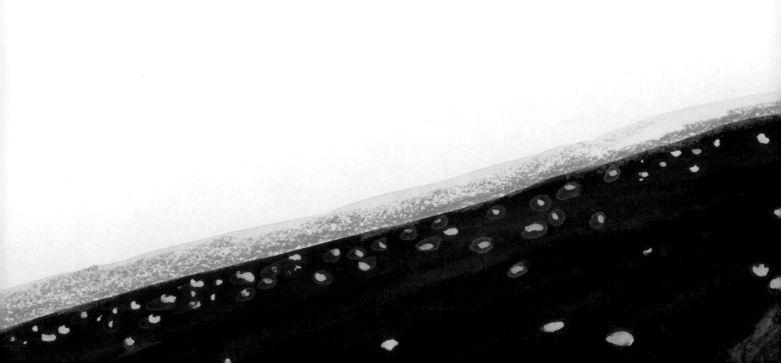

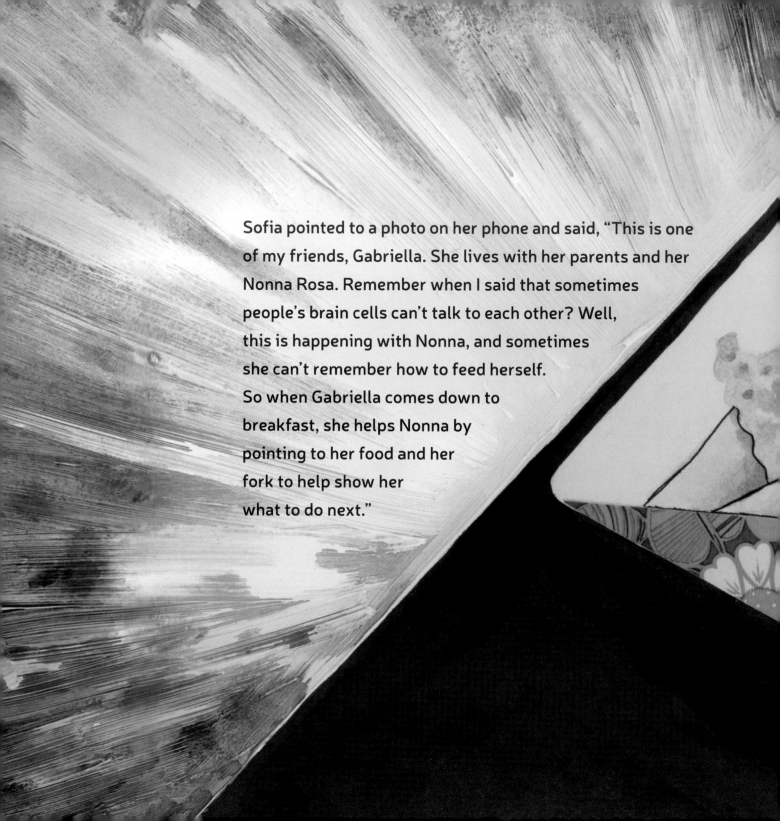

Sofia pointed to a photo on her phone and said, "This is one of my friends, Gabriella. She lives with her parents and her Nonna Rosa. Remember when I said that sometimes people's brain cells can't talk to each other? Well, this is happening with Nonna, and sometimes she can't remember how to feed herself. So when Gabriella comes down to breakfast, she helps Nonna by pointing to her food and her fork to help show her what to do next."

Sofia continued, "Another
thing that can happen when
brain cells aren't able to communicate
is that it can be hard for people to
understand words — or find the right
ones to use. That's the challenge
for my friend Luna and her Tio Pablo.
When Tio is having a hard time understanding
her, Luna talks to him in short sentences and
doesn't rush their conversations. Sometimes, she
even uses pictures to help show him what she is saying."

"My friend Mark's Grandpa Ted has a type of dementia that can cause him to get scared very easily," Sofia said as she scrolled to another photo. "Mark makes sure he doesn't startle him by always approaching him from the front so Grandpa can SEE Mark before he talks with him.

"Also, Grandpa Ted sometimes sees things that others can't or says things that Mark knows are not correct," Sofia explained. "If Mark notices this, he remembers that Grandpa's brain believes it IS correct, so he doesn't argue with Grandpa but tells him he loves him and steps out of the room to find an adult to help Grandpa."

Sofia continued, "My friend Kamar's Nanna Ruth has a type of dementia that makes it difficult for her hands and legs to work like she wants them to, so it takes a long time to do even the smallest movement. When Kamar is helping Nanna get ready for church, he waits patiently for her to button her coat and walk down the hallway. He knows she still likes to do things for herself, even if it takes her a long time."

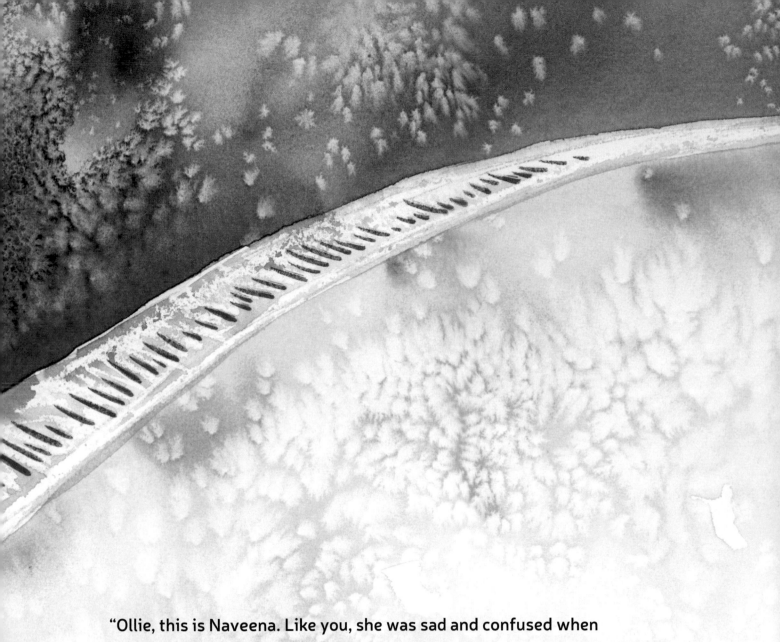

"Ollie, this is Naveena. Like you, she was sad and confused when she would visit her Dada-Ji and he wouldn't remember her," said Sofia.

"Did Naveena get scared when Dada-Ji didn't know her name, too?" Ollie asked.

"Yes, she did," said Sofia. "But then Naveena learned
that whenever she visits him, she can still be his friend.
Each time she visits, and he doesn't know her, she introduces
herself like she is a NEW friend. Often, she plays music he loves
and sings his favorite songs, even if he doesn't remember them.
Sometimes, Naveena just sits quietly and holds his hand, watches TV,
or looks at photo albums, just like a good friend."

"Do her visits with her grandpa always go well?"
Ollie wondered.

"Not always, Ollie. Even if we do ALL the things we've learned and try our VERY best to make things go right, some visits might not go well because our loved one is just having a hard day," Sofia explained.

"When this happens, watch for signs that Grandpa Walt isn't comfortable, and you can

• ask him what he needs,

• ask someone who helps care for him — like me — what might make him feel better, or

• simply give him some time alone.

But most of all, you can remember how much you love him and all the great memories you've made together. This will help you look forward to the next visit."

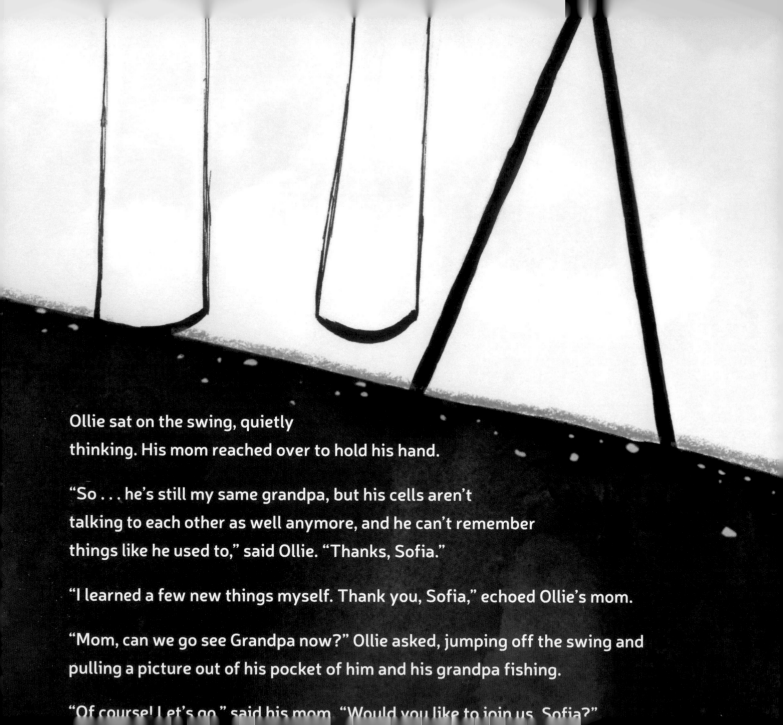

Ollie sat on the swing, quietly
thinking. His mom reached over to hold his hand.

"So . . . he's still my same grandpa, but his cells aren't
talking to each other as well anymore, and he can't remember
things like he used to," said Ollie. "Thanks, Sofia."

"I learned a few new things myself. Thank you, Sofia," echoed Ollie's mom.

"Mom, can we go see Grandpa now?" Ollie asked, jumping off the swing and
pulling a picture out of his pocket of him and his grandpa fishing.

"Of course! Let's go," said his mom. "Would you like to join us, Sofia?"

As Ollie stood in front of Grandpa Walt holding up the picture, he remembered what Sofia had taught him. Ollie extended his hand saying, "Hi! My name is Ollie. I like to fish."

"Hi! I'm Walt. Where do you fish, Ollie?" asked his grandpa.

Sofia stepped forward and asked, "Can I take a picture of you both?"

"Sure!" said Ollie, putting his arm around his grandpa's shoulders. "Mr. Walt, say 'fishing!'"

As Sofia snapped the picture, she smiled knowing that Ollie and Grandpa Walt had found a new friendship, and Ollie had the knowledge to help it last.

YOU HAVE THE POWER TO SEE

My mind is changing but I am still here

What you see has no resemblance to the fabric of my life

See beyond the frayed remnants left today

See instead the richness in the colors of the threads —
it is in them you'll know the woman I was,
the accomplishments I made, the legacies I leave,
the people I loved, the love I need,
and the gifts I still have to give this world

I cannot tell you these but YOU have the power to see

Suzanne Bottum-Jones

RESOURCES
Commonly asked questions:
What is dementia and how is it different from Alzheimer's disease?

How does dementia affect the brain?

What causes the different forms of dementia?

What is the diagnostic process for dementia?

What are the treatments for Alzheimer's and other dementias?

What supports are available for families and caregivers?

How do I get involved in clinical trials?

For more information regarding these and other questions about Alzheimer's and other related dementias please visit:

US Department of Health and Human Services
National Institute on Aging: www.nia.nih.gov
- Go to Health Information then click on Alzheimer's and Related Dementias
- Alzheimer's Disease Education and Referral Center: www.nia.nih.gov/alzheimers

National Associations
Alzheimer's Association: www.alz.org

Us Against Alzheimer's: www.usagainstalzheimers.org

Alzheimer's Foundation of America: https://alzfdn.org

Lewy Body Dementia Association: www.lbda.org

The Association for Frontotemporal Degeneration: www.theaftd.org

Brain Injury Association of America: www.biausa.org

National Association for Down Syndrome: www.nads.org

Bright Focus Foundation: www.brightfocus.org

In addition to the above resources, please contact your local community aging resources for local services within your community.

Wisconsin Residents: In Suzanne's home state of Wisconsin, she has worked directly with the following resources regarding clinical trials and encourages you to contact them for more information:
Wisconsin Alzheimer's Institute: www.wai.wisc.edu

Wisconsin Alzheimer's Disease Research Center: www.adrc.wisc.edu

ABOUT THE AUTHOR

Suzanne Bottum-Jones is a registered nurse with over 15 years of experience working with the management of behaviors and psychological symptoms associated with dementia, brain injury, and other forms of cognitive impairment. She is a nationally recognized speaker, behavioral consultant, educator, and advocate who works to encourage health professionals and caregivers to include behavioral strategies designed to move beyond pharmacologic-only interventions. Suzanne is currently involved in developing and piloting ABAIT (Agitated Behavioral Assessment and Intervention Tools), a software platform designed to merge with electronic medical records that assist health care professionals and caregivers to improve quality of life and health outcomes for dementia patients. Suzanne Bottum-Jones resides in rural Wisconsin with her family on a five-generation farm. She loves sharing the beauty of the farm with friends, caring for her family, and helping families experiencing difficulties with dementia. Her motto in life has been to *live gently, love passionately, and choose joy everyday.*

ABOUT THE ILLUSTRATOR

Aaron Boyd is an award-winning Wisconsin born illustrator of children's books and games for over 20 years. Aaron has illustrated over 30 books focusing mostly on animal and multicultural themes. Additionally, he has a great love for his home state and enjoys helping to bring local stories to bookshelves.